PU
GRAND

Reeta Dutta Gupta worked as a ~~......~~ ~~,~~
to the early 1990s and contributed articles, reviews and interviews to the *Times of India*, *Hindustan Times* and other national papers. She fell in love with the wonders of the African wilderness while reading a book on it and later lived in Africa for several years. Her first children's stories set in Africa appeared in two anthologies: *The Nose Doctor* and *Best of Target Stories*. She has published two books for children—*Midnight Train and Other Ghost Stories* and *How Mnjini Became a Magician and Other African Tales*—and a short picture book *Monuments of India* for the very young. Her other books include short biographies of Rabindranath Tagore and Salim Ali, and *I Am Radha*, a work of fiction.

Grandmother's Tales

REETA DUTTA GUPTA

Illustrations by
Vandana Bist

PUFFIN BOOKS

PUFFIN BOOKS
Penguin Books India (P) Ltd., 11 Community Centre, Panchsheel
Park, New Delhi 110017, India
Penguin Books Ltd., 80 Strand, London WC2R 0RL, UK
Penguin Group Inc., 375 Hudson Street, New York, NY 10014, USA
Penguin Books Australia Ltd., 250 Camberwell Road, Camberwell,
Victoria 3124, Australia
Penguin Books Canada Ltd., 10 Alcorn Avenue, Suite 300, Toronto,
Ontario M4V 3B2, Canada
Penguin Books (NZ) Ltd., Cnr Rosedale & Airborne Roads, Albany,
Auckland, New Zealand
Penguin Books (South Africa) (Pty) Ltd., 24 Sturdee Avenue,
Rosebank 2196, South Africa

First published in Puffin by Penguin Books India 2003

Copyright © Reeta Dutta Gupta 2003

All rights reserved

10 9 8 7 6 5 4 3 2 1

Typeset in ACaslon Regular by Eleven Arts, Delhi-35

Printed at Baba Barkhanath Printers, New Delhi

CONTENTS

In fond memory of my grandmother—
Labanya Prabha—for her story books,
loads of sweets, and the many
rhyming poems she scibbled on postcards

Author's Note

Have you ever asked your Grandma to tell you a story?

Well, grandmothers and grandaunts—be they ancient or modern—love to narrate tales to wide-eyed children. And the little ones love these stories—stories of crazy ghosts, nitwit demons and wicked rakshashis with crooked, hairy legs and long, unclean teeth; stories of talkative animals who behave like wise or foolish men, and dreamy-eyed princes and princesses, who so readily fall in love! Actually, it is not just children who love stories. Most adults enjoy a well-told tale even though they may have grown a middle-age paunch and grey hairs.

Since very, very ancient times, stories have been told and heard for pleasure. It was only much later that they began to be recorded in books. After darkness fell, perhaps ancient people gathered in their cave-shelters or the villagers—the weaver, the barber, the merchant and the boatman—sat by the blazing fireside outside their mud huts after a hard day's work to relax and listen to fantastic stories about witches and ghouls, about simple village folk like themselves, and about the animals of the fields and forests. These ancient oral tales are sometimes called grandmother's tales. Grandmothers told these stories that they themselves had had heard as children from their elders or cooks and servants, to entertain the young at mealtimes or at bedtime to put them to sleep.

In these folktales animals and trees and even stones are speaking beings like humans, for it is a world where all are important. Here the hardworking, the witty, the clever and the one who knows how to love win in the end over the ugly evil being, out to gobble up the good. These stories amuse, please and advise, but above all they lend wings to the imagination. In olden days when ships sailed from the ports of ancient Bharat and caravans left carrying cotton and gold and spices, the stories too went places as traders who heard these tales retold them and every time told them a little differently with new local additions and changes. They are stories, you see, that are as much fun to retell and recreate as they are to listen to. Many tales travelled to Europe through Persia; even within the country, some stories have several versions.

I too have enjoyed recreating these tales for you. I have given new names to characters who had none, sprinkled a little naughtiness here and there for fun, rewritten endings to suit our times, and, in the case of *Hiraman*, recreated a whole scene to give a modern twist to an old tale. In short, I have told these age-old stories in my own way. And Vandana has made many of the bizarre scenes and crazy characters come alive with her superb ink-drawings just to bring you loads of joy. I hope you will have as much fun reading this book as we—and Udayan and Ajanta at Puffin Books—did bringing it to you!

New Delhi   Reeta Dutta Gupta

July 2003

Magic Box

Golden Stick, Silver Stick

A long, long time ago, when the sky was the colour of sapphire and white mother-of-pearl clouds sailed in the heavens and the forest trees had leaves like bright green emeralds and the birds had wings as if studded with many precious gems—red rubies, yellow sapphire, black pearl and blue diamonds—there lived a handsome young prince in the kingdom of Roopsagar. He was not interested in statecraft. He did not dream of becoming the king some day. Enchanted by the colours of the wilderness, he loved nothing better than to ride into the forests with his three friends, the sons of the prime minister, the treasurer and the commander-in-chief of the king's twenty-thousand strong army, and revel in nature's beauty.

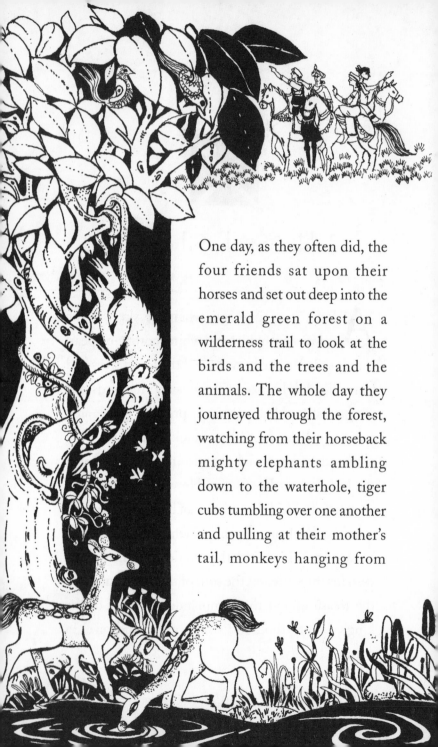

One day, as they often did, the four friends sat upon their horses and set out deep into the emerald green forest on a wilderness trail to look at the birds and the trees and the animals. The whole day they journeyed through the forest, watching from their horseback mighty elephants ambling down to the waterhole, tiger cubs tumbling over one another and pulling at their mother's tail, monkeys hanging from trees or somersaulting on the grass, herds of deer gambolling upon a golden field and many, many jewel-winged birds and sweet-scented wild flowers. 'Ah! This is paradise!' they exclaimed. The forest was indeed lovely and all day long, the four young men enjoyed themselves thoroughly. And just before the sun, a crimson ball of fire, was about to set behind the stretch of broad-leafed sal trees, the four friends decided to bathe in the ice-cool cascading waters of a forest stream that raced over smooth round diamond-white pebbles making a gentle murmur. Then, as they came out of the stream and tied their turbans and their belts—it was quite dark by then—a huge rakshashi with thick dishevelled hair that fell all over her face and bulbous eyes that looked like two big white eggs and teeth long like radishes, suddenly appeared before them. Screaming and shrieking, she sang in a nasal tone at the top of her voice:

> Haow! Maow! Khaow!
> Gulp! Gobble! Swallow!
> Tender, delicious meat
> Of four young men so sweet!
> Haow! Maow! Khaow!

No sooner had she finished her song, she gobbled, gulped and swallowed up the sons of the prime minister, the treasurer and the commander-in-chief of the king's twenty-thousand strong army. And just as she was about to make a grab at the terror-stricken young prince, he jumped upon his horse, which was a flying horse, and at the speed of lightning flew into the sapphire-blue sky. The rakshashi now became furious at the prince's escape and in a fit of rage, she tore up some of her thick, curly, matted hair and pulled out a peepal tree by its roots. Then, one by one, she gulped down the three horses of the three friends of the prince. And screaming and shrieking, and bellowing and howling, she ran off deep into the darkness, her tousled hair flying in the air, her bulbous eyes rolling furiously and her long radish-like teeth rattling and clattering.

It was midnight now and the young prince was tired and weary of gliding through the air seated upon his flying horse. His father's palace was still miles away, so he decided to come down to the earth to rest in the forest for the night and resume his journey back home early next morning. But just as the horse landed and the prince dismounted, he heard the rakshashi

come screaming and shrieking after him, bellowing and howling and singing in a nasal tone:

Haow! Maow! Khaow!
Gulp! Gobble! Swallow!
Tender, delicious meat
Of a young prince so sweet!
Haow! Maow! Khaow!

Trembling with fright, the prince fell to his knees and with folded hands prayed to a nearby mango tree to save his life. 'Tree, tree! I've loved you well. Please save my life.' And the kind mango tree replied, 'Come, my dear prince, come and hide in my trunk.' (You see, trees are most kind and anyone will speak to you if you speak to them lovingly.)

And the prince, who was very loving, hugged the tree and exclaimed, 'O, kind tree, thank you, so much!' At once the tree opened its trunk for the prince to step in and then became whole again.

Now, when the rakshashi reached the tree and once again failed to catch the prince, she swallowed the prince's horse and began to beat the tree violently with her thick club-like hands, kick at it with her hairy legs and tear down the branches and the leaves of the tree. But still, the tree refused to give up the prince.

The rakshashi now threatened to pull out the tree by its roots and was about to do so, when a golden dawn broke out in the eastern sky. Quickly the demoness changed herself into a maiden and deftly covered the ugly hunch upon her back with her long silken hair and hid her crooked, hairy, spindly legs

and her patchy skin like that of a field lizard.
Then sitting beneath the tree she began to
weep piteously. She knew that every morning
the king of the nearby kingdom of Rampur

passed through the forest on his way to the temple by the river. Though she was nothing much to look at—remember all that she hid under her hair, petticoat and her sari—she was sure she could make the old king fall in love with her by shedding pearl-like tears.

And sure enough, the king soon came riding into the forest and when he saw the maiden sitting all by herself and weeping, he was moved by her tears and fell in love with her. He took her along to his palace and made her his bride, little knowing that the maiden was in reality a horrid, stinking, ugly rakshashi.

The wicked rakshashi queen now had only one aim—to gulp down the young prince who had taken shelter in the trunk of the mango tree. So, she began to plot and scheme and feigned a strange illness. She put some dry sticks and round pebbles underneath the mattress of her bed so that it made a rattling sound whenever she turned. And she said to the king, 'My king, you love me not. Here I lie in bed ill with a disease that makes my bones rattle and clack and you do nothing to save me. If you love me well, send your men into the forest at once to chop down the very mango tree under which you had found me. I shall have a powder made after burning down its wood, and that alone can cure me of my illness.

The king now sent his men into the forest to chop down the mango tree. The tree, sensing danger, asked the prince to squeeze into its biggest mango so that the wind could carry it away into the far distance. And sure enough, the mango was blown away, away, away and fell into a river with a splash. In the river, there lived a huge rohu fish. The prince said to the fish, 'Kind fish, give me shelter. For a rakshashi is after my blood.' And the fish gobbled up the mango with the prince inside it.

Once again, the prince had escaped. The rakshashi queen was furious. In the dark of the night she munched away the king's goats and cows. Then, she ran into the king's chamber scratching her itching spindly legs and shrieking and shedding crocodile's tears said, 'I no longer need the powder of the mango tree. What I want now is a piece of the biggest rohu fish to cure me of my illness.'

 The foolish, old king, who could never guess the truth, at once commanded his men to go and net the fish. The fish, sensing danger, said to the prince, 'I shall swim and take you to the mouth of the river. Where the river falls into the sea there lives a kind oyster. The oyster shall give you shelter.'

The rohu fish at once swam to the oyster and the kind oyster opened its shell and the prince stepped into it. Like this, the prince lived in the oyster for days and weeks and months. Then, one day, a peasant woman came to bathe at the mouth of the river. Just as she took a dip in the waters, her foot touched the oyster, making the shell open up. The woman was surprised to see a handsome prince inside the oyster and more so when he told her that he was hiding from a rakshashi, who was determined to gobble him up.

Hearing the prince's story, the kind woman invited him to her hut. 'Do not worry, young prince. Come with me to my hut and I will give you shelter,' she said.

The prince followed the woman to her house and there he lived happily for days. One day, when the prince decided to leave for his father's palace, the rakshashi queen, using her special power to sense things, got wind of the prince's whereabouts. Shedding crocodile tears and turning on her bed to make it rattle and clack, she cried, 'O, my bones! My rattling bones! Neither the powder of the mango tree,  nor a piece of the biggest rohu fish can cure me of my illness. My king, bring me the young prince who lives in the hut of a peasant woman. For he is brave and he alone can ride through the forest full of dangers and beyond to the kingdom of my relatives. There, he will find a sky-piercing tower guarded by a gang of rakshashis. In the tower is a small golden box, containing magic potions that alone can cure me of my illness.'

'Your wish is my command,' said the foolish king, little suspecting his wicked queen. At once he sent his men on horses and elephants to look for the young prince who lived in a peasant woman's hut and soon, on finding him, brought him to the king.

'Ride into the forest, young prince, and beyond to the land of my queen's relatives,' commanded the king. 'Yonder, you shall find a sky-piercing tower guarded by a gang of rakshashis and in the tower is a golden box. Go, brave man, and get me the golden box, for it contains a magic potion that shall cure my queen of her illness that makes her bones rattle and clack. If you do as I say, you shall be rewarded. If not, beheaded you certainly will be!'

With a shudder, the prince understood at once that the queen was none other than the rakshashi who longed to make a tasty meal of him. But before the prince could say a word, he was put upon a horse and the horse raced with him into the deep forest.

Through mango groves and forests of sal trees, and past titanic banyan, peepal and jackfruit trees, the horse raced on and on over hedges, ditches and many a sprawling field. Then, at last, it came to a halt before the sky-piercing tower. With trembling knees and bated breath the prince stood wondering what to do next. Any moment now, he thought, the rakshashis would come rushing out of the tower to eat him up. Yet, should he turn back and flee without the golden box, he was sure to lose his head.

Finally, gathering up courage—for he was a brave prince—he walked into the tower through the gate. To his surprise it seemed completely deserted. Not a sound did he hear. Inside the tower was such a dreadful silence that a shiver went down his spine. But as the door to one of the rooms stood a little ajar, he slipped in through it, just to see what was there. The room was empty but it led to another room and to another room and to yet another room. And then, in an inner room, upon a huge lotus he found a beautiful young girl. She was in such deep sleep that she did not seem even to breathe. A sweet perfume of jasmine wafted through the room from her pearl-white body. She was so lovely to look at that a soft, golden light radiated from her face. The prince was certain she was no ordinary girl, but a princess. Spellbound, he at once fell in love with her as he sat down beside her to admire her enchanting face. Forgetting that a gang of rakshashis guarded the tower, and could come rushing in any moment to gobble him up, he sat wondering as to when she would wake up.

Like this, hours passed. Still, when the beautiful young girl did not stir, the prince decided to wake her up himself. Slowly, he bent down his head and kissed her rosy red lips. But she did not wake up. He called her softly and whispered sweet words into her delicate ears pierced with rubies and diamonds. Still the girl did not wake up. Now, he gently shook her and just as he did so, he noticed a silver stick lying at her head and a golden stick at her tiny feet. He picked

up the sticks wondering what these were and began to play with them. Then, he put the sticks back. But he had forgotten which stick had been at the girl's head and which at her feet. He now put the golden stick at her head and the silver stick at her feet and just as he did so, like magic the girl woke up. The prince took the beautiful lady in his arms and she told him that she was indeed a princess and that the gang of rakshashis who lived in the sky-piercing tower had made her their prisoner. They put her to sleep by putting the golden stick at her feet and the silver stick at her head whenever they left for the forest for their meals. And when they returned, they woke her up by placing the sticks in the reverse order. The rakshashis had killed her parents, the king and queen, and all her relatives, and taken over her father's tower. But as she was so lovely to look at, they had taken a great fancy to her exquisite beauty and had kept her alive and played with her like a doll when they returned from the forest. But every morning, when they went off into the forest, they always put her to sleep.

The prince now told the princess how he had been sent to the tower by the rakshashi queen to collect the golden box so that her relatives would kill him. The princess knew about the golden box and showed him where it was kept and told him that the box contained magic potions which protected the lives of all the rakshashis. If ever the potion was spilled on to the ground, all the rakshashis would fall to the ground and die. That was why when they were away, they put her to sleep.

The prince was more than delighted by what the princess had told him. He quickly took the golden box and spilled some potions on the ground. At once, all the rakshashis who lived in the tower came back from the forest howling and screaming. Some fell down at the gate. Some fainted. Some rolled on the ground in great pain. The prince quickly spilled some more potions and soon the entire gang of rakshashis had dropped down dead.

The prince now mounted his horse with the princess carrying the golden box and rode back to the rakshashi queen's palace. And just as the she saw him come in with the princess carrying the golden box, with a terrifying howl she assumed her real form and came charging at the prince. But before she could make a grab at him, the prince took the golden box from the princess and quickly emptied it on the ground. At once, screaming and shrieking, the rakshashi fell down dead.

The king's eyes were opened at last. He now saw that his queen was a terrible rakshashi who had been gobbling away his goats and cows in the stealth of the night and he was glad to have got rid of her. He rewarded the prince with riches and a flying horse. Then, on a day when the sky was the bluest blue upon which sailed white, mother-of-pearl clouds and jewel-winged birds flew about singing songs and emerald-green leaves gently moved in the wind, the king sent the prince and his lovely princess back to the kingdom of Roopsagar.

Hiraman, the Singing Bird

Day after day, month after month and season after season, a bird-catcher came into the forest with a net and sticks quoted with glue to trick the little unsuspecting birds into becoming his captives. The birds of the forest were now in a quandary, for the bird-catcher caught them by the dozens and sold them in the marketplace to perverse little boys and girls who liked keeping pet birds in cages. The parakeets, the mynas, the budgerigars and a host of other forest birds lived in mortal fear of being caught any day. They were so fearful of falling into the bird-catcher's net or getting stuck on his glue stick that they gave up singing their songs. This made the trees and the flowers and the butterflies, oh, so very sad. After all, what is a forest without birdsong?

One day, when Hiraman-tota, the beautiful grass-green parakeet with a rose-pink and black collar band, a long pointed tail, and a beak as red as ruby, found his companions missing—they had been captured, imprisoned in small cages and taken to the city— little drops of tears rolled down from his bird eyes, and he took a solemn vow to somehow stop this deplorable trade. Birds are for the open skies! Birds have extraordinary wings that made even men want to fly! Of all the creatures in the world, who else has wings to take to the blue skies and fly across oceans, deserts and dales? And what a shame that these soaring, freedom-loving birds should be put behind the bars of a tiny cage where they could not even stretch out their wings! Hiraman now decided to do something to make the bird-catcher give up his evil trade. And so, the next day, when the man came into the forest, Hiraman spoke to him. 'Bird-catcher, bird-catcher, I'm Hiraman-tota. Tell me, why do you catch birds?' he asked.

'To sell them and make some money,' the man replied candidly.

'I shall help you to find riches. Will you then stop catching my comrades?'

'If only I and my wife have enough money to buy our meals, I shall give up catching birds, Hiraman,' the bird-catcher promised.

'You shall have the money not only to buy your meals but also to buy a house and a boat and two bullocks if you please. Instead of catching birds, could you not become a farmer, or a blacksmith or a silversmith, or anything else? Oh, please spare us, for we birds are not meant to live in a cage. We are birds of the open skies! We have wings!'

The bird-catcher was surprised by what the bird said. 'This is an extraordinary bird,' he thought and asked, 'What makes you think you can find me riches?'

'Just leave that to me!' Hiraman said. Saying so, he flew down from the tree and perched on the bird-catcher's shoulder. 'Take me to your home,' he commanded.

Through the dense forest, the bird-catcher walked along the winding forest pathway back to his hut with Hiraman sitting on his shoulder. When he reached his hut, his wife, who stood waiting for him at the door, her arms akimbo, shouted, 'What is this green little patch I see on your shoulder?'

'It's a bird, wife!' said the man.

'A bird? You mean you've brought home just one bird? And what shall we do with a single bird?' the wife screamed. 'What shall we sell in the market today? What shall we eat tonight?' And before the bird-catcher could utter a single word, the wife made a swift grab at Hiraman saying, 'Let's roast this little bird and eat it tonight with red, hot chilly sauce.' But Hiraman quickly flew up on to a bamboo pole, which stood in the courtyard, and in the sweetest voice crooned, 'Bird-catcher's wife, bird-catcher's wife, why does your husband catch birds?'

'If he does not catch birds, what shall we eat? What shall we sell to make some money?' the woman asked candidly.

'I shall help you to get riches if your husband gives up catching my friends!' Hiraman replied.

'If only I and my husband have the money to afford two square meals a day, we shall surely give up catching birds,' the bird-catcher's wife too promised.

'You shall have the money not only to buy your meals but also to buy a house and a boat and two bullocks if you please. Instead of catching birds, do farming, or any thing! But oh, please spare us, for we birds are not meant to live in a cage. We are birds of the open skies! We have wings!'

The woman was both surprised and pleased to hear what Hiraman said. 'Find us the riches you promise and my husband shall give up catching birds,' she said.

'Tomorrow morning, as soon as it is dawn, take me to the king's palace,' Hiraman commanded, and sitting on the bamboo pole, he fell fast asleep.

The next morning, as soon as the sun was up, Hiraman began to sing a sweet song. And all at once the bird-catcher and his wife woke up. Listening to Hiraman's sweet song, they were simply enchanted. 'It's an extraordinary bird!' they exclaimed.

'I've never heard a parakeet sing so sweetly,' the wife said. And then, with the bird perched upon the man's shoulder, the three left for the king's palace.

That morning the king was in his chamber parleying with the queen. But when he saw the bird, he at once fell in love with the parakeet. He was a great bird lover and he was delighted to see Hiraman. Given a choice, he would have become an ornithologist. (My sweet children, that big word means one who studies birds.) But he had to wear his father's crown and rule as a king. Nevertheless, he liked to spend long hours in the forest watching birds and listening to their calls. So when Hiraman began to sing a sweet *teewit-teewit* song, the king was beside himself with joy. 'My good man and woman, what is the price of this bird? I shall love to have it,' he said grinning from ear to ear.

'A thousand gold coins!' Hiraman exclaimed and flew up to the king and perched on his shoulder. The bird-catcher and his wife could not believe their ears. 'Yes, yes! A thousand gold coins!' they chorused.

The kind-hearted king, who was so delighted to have the bird come and sit upon his shoulder, at once said, 'I shall give you a thousand gold coins each!'

'O great king!' the bird-catcher exclaimed, 'You shall be grateful to us one day for bringing you this bird. Just as he has brought us luck, so will he prove lucky for you some day. For this is no ordinary bird but a magic tota!' Then, singing and whistling and walking hand-in-hand the bird-catcher and his wife returned home and on their way they bought laddus and many other kinds of yummy-yummy sweets to celebrate the happy occasion. And they made great plans as to what they would do with all that money.

Now, the king was so fascinated with the bird—for Hiraman sang ever so sweetly — that he summoned his men and ordered a special gold cage studded with precious gems to be made for the bird. But Hiraman protested, 'A bird in a cage, my king, puts God in a rage! Birds have wings, let them soar in the skies.'

'O, wise bird!' the king exclaimed. 'Your wish is my command! From henceforth, you shall always be a free bird!'

Hiraman was delighted. He thanked the king and told him that he should have the freedom to go into the forest whenever he wanted to and if ever the king called for him, he would come flying in at once and sing him a song.

So Hiraman lived in the palace and he travelled to the forest and whenever the king called, he came flying in to greet him. And all day long the king sighed for Hiraman.

'O, my Hiraman! O, my Hiraman!' he said all day and sometimes even in his sleep in the middle of the night, and Hiraman, the beautiful grass-green parakeet with a rose-pink and black collar band, a long pointed tail, and a beak as red as ruby, came flying through the forest to perch upon the king's shoulder. And the king would say, 'Sing my bird, sing,'—and even in the middle of the night Hiraman would begin his sweet *teewit-teewit* song, so full of melody that the king, intoxicated by the music, closed his eyes, swayed his head rhythmically, clapped his hands like a little boy, and exclaimed, 'Ah ha! Ah ha! Waaaaah!

'Waaaaah!' the angry queen would mock the king and make faces behind his back—horrid, ugly faces—and call him a nincompoop. (Now my children, here's another big word. Find out the meaning. But don't you be one!) She was very jealous of Hiraman, of whom the king had grown so very fond. 'Ever since this foolish bird has come into the palace, the king spends all his time listening to the bird sing its stupid *teewit-teewit* song. He has no time for me!' the queen would often gripe and grumble and then, making a terrifying face, she would swear, 'Wait till I wrench off the saucy little parakeet's head one of these days! Wait till I roast Hiraman alive and serve him to the king with red, hot chilly sauce for his lunch!'

Now, no one in the palace knew that the queen was actually a hideous, stinking, revolting rakshashi who loved to nibble and munch and crunch in the middle of the night juicy cockroaches and frogs that tasted like candy to her, and snakes, salamanders and lizards, which she sucked like lollipops holding them by their tails. Day after day, year after year she had been gobbling up the creatures of the forest—birds, deer, jackals, foxes, wolves and even tigers by the dozens—all in the deep dark night. And when she became bored eating the forest animals, she turned herself into a beautiful princess just to marry the king, so that she could eat up his horses and elephants in the dark of the night. Every night, after the king went to bed, she walked out quietly, resumed her form of a female demon and swallowed up live elephants and horses one after the other. And yet, because of her special power—which all rakshashis have—she remained slim and trim and never ever burped or belched before the king nor anyone else giving away the odour of elephant meat. So no one in the palace ever suspected her to be a demoness in a woman's disguise. If the king had a passion for birds—in fact, he loved all animals and was most kind to them and gave out injunctions that his subjects must love and respect all animals—the rakshashi queen detested them just as much. If she cared for animals it was only to gobble them up as her meal.

One evening, when Hiraman flew into the king's chamber, perched on his shoulder and began to pipe a sweet melody and the king exclaimed, 'Ah ha! Ah ha! Waaaah!' the rakshashi queen vowed to soon finish off Hiraman. Green with jealousy, she hatched a wicked plot to kill the bird.

One day, when the king was out in the forest watching birds and taking down notes like a naturalist, the queen called for Hiraman and asked him to come and perch upon her shoulder. Then in the sweetest of voices, she asked, 'Tell, me my sweet Hiraman, who is the loveliest lady of all?'

Little suspecting the queen's intention, Hiraman at once came and sat upon the queen's shoulder to take a close look at her face to see if she was the loveliest lady of all. But to his horror he noticed the queen's ugly whiskers (some female rakshashis, my sweet children, have whiskers like cats!) which the queen did her best to cover up with blotches of paint and powder. So Hiraman exclaimed, 'You my queen are not the loveliest of all! Beyond the forest, behind the hills, across the sprawling fields there is a garden house with crystal doors. There lives a maiden who loves birds and beasts. Her cheeks are soft like rose petals.

Her hair is beautiful like the night stringed with pearls. Her skin is as smooth as sandalwood paste and her rosy lips which sport no whiskers are fit to be kissed by a king! It is she who is the loveliest of all!'

Just as Hiraman uttered these words, the rakshashi queen in a fit of rage let out a terrifying cry and assuming her terrible form with one swat of her ugly, twisted, hairy hand tried to quash Hiraman to death like a little fly. But Hiraman escaped swiftly in the nick of time and flew off into the forest. The rakshashi, burning with hatred and turning greener and greener and greener with jealousy, finally dropped down dead. (You see, jealousy is indeed killing!) And as she fell down dead at that very moment the king returned to his chamber and got the shock of his life. For there at his feet lay the rakshashi queen in her demon form. Horrified, the king ran out into the forest and called for Hiraman, for whenever he felt under the weather or got into a blue fit or something made him sad, he called for Hiraman to sing to him and make him feel well again. The bird at once returned to the king to sing to him but before he began his song, he told the king all that had happened. When Hiraman finished his song, which, sure enough cured the king of his great shock, the king asked dreamily, 'Where did you say, my bird, lived the loveliest maiden?'

'I shall take you to her, if you like,' Hiraman replied. 'She lives far, far away, beyond the forest, behind the hills, across the sprawling fields in a garden house with crystal doors.'

The king now asked Hiraman to take him at once to the loveliest maiden. Hiraman suggested that the king should go to meet the maiden riding on his flying horse. He also asked him to  order the royal silversmith to make a thousand silver pebbles. When the pebbles were ready, the king took a bag full of them and mounting his flying horse flew into the sky. Hiraman too soared into the sky and led the way. At last they reached the garden house with crystal doors, where lived the loveliest maiden. There they alighted.

'Now tie your horse behind the tree and give me your bag of silver pebbles. Then, go and climb to the top of that lofty tree and remain there till I ask you to come down,' Hiraman commanded. The king did exactly as he was told. Hiraman now took the silver pebbles in his beak and dropped them one by one around the tree and along the garden path leading to the maiden's house with crystal doors.

Every evening, the loveliest maiden came out through

her crystal doors to feed the birds. That evening, when she opened her door, she saw the silver pebbles lying along the garden path. 'Now what on earth are these?' the maiden wondered, picking up the pebbles as she followed their trail that led up to the tree where the king and Hiraman sat upon a branch hiding. And when she came up to the tree, Hiraman burst into his sweet *teewit-teewit* song.

Enchanted by the melody, the maiden exclaimed, 'Ah ha! Ah ha! Waaaaah!'—just as the king would exclaim when Hiraman sang—and then she closed her eyes, swayed her head rhythmically, keeping beat with the melody as long as the music went on. When the music stopped, she opened her eyes to see which bird sang so sweetly. But instead, she found the king standing before her with the beautiful singing bird perched on his shoulder. Hiraman had asked the king to climb down from the tree while he sang and go and stand before the maiden. The maiden, on seeing the handsome young king, stood spellbound before him. She had heard of the king's great love for birds and animals and she had always wished to meet the king. Now she found him standing right at her doorstep!

Kneeling down before the maiden, the king said, 'My lovely girl, your beauty is as enchanting as the goodness of your heart! Hiraman tells me you're a bird lover just as I am. And I saw with my own eyes how much you appreciated my Hiraman's song! Will you be my queen?' And saying so, the king offered the maiden a beautiful ring made of diamonds, rubies, pearls and emeralds set in gold, which he had taken along with him.

Graciously accepting the ring, the maiden replied, 'I will marry you, my king.' The king stood up now and kissed the maiden and then sitting upon the royal flying horse with Hiraman perched on the maiden's shoulder, they flew over the forest and the hills and the sprawling fields and reached the king's palace. Amidst much rejoicing, dancing and singing and royal feasting, the king married his new queen. To mark the happy occasion and honour Hiraman, the king and the queen jointly passed a decree forbidding men and women, girls and boys to ever keep a bird locked in a cage.

'And if ever I catch a naughty little girl or boy breaking my law, I shall surely cut off the child's nose!' the king warned.

And the queen exclaimed, 'Birds have wings and they must fly. Birds are for the blue skies!'

Sukhu and Dukhu

S ukhu and Dukhu were two sisters and each was like the shadow of the other. Wherever Sukhu went, Dukhu followed. And wherever Dukhu went, Sukhu was sure to go with her. Yet, though they loved one another much, the two were always at loggerheads. If Sukhu said, 'Sister Dukhu, let's go and help mother in the kitchen,' Dukhu was sure to say, 'Nah, don't be such a goodie goodie, Sukhu! Mother hasn't asked for help. Let's go out and play hop-scotch in the garden instead.' And again, if ever Sukhu wanted to play, Dukhu would say, 'Sister Sukhu, I'm in no mood to play; let's go into our neighbour's garden to steal flowers and guavas.' Sometimes Sukhu was tempted to do all the naughty things that Dukhu asked her to do but in the end she stopped just short of doing it, saying, 'No, no, we mustn't steal . . . we mustn't lie . . . we mustn't disobey!'

Sukhu and Dukhu were the very opposites in their looks too. Sukhu was plain and simple with an ordinary countenance, while Dukhu was proud and vainglorious. And while Sukhu was kind and loving and helpful, Dukhu was selfish to the core of her heart.

One day, Sukhu and Dukhu's father, who was a weaver, said to his daughters, 'My girls, I've some work in the village. While I'm out, could you please do some spinning for me?' Saying so, he left, while his wife got busy with her housework. Now, instead of sitting down to spin, Dukhu threw a tantrum, saying, 'Sister

Sukhu, I don't like spinning. Let's go out into the forest and climb every tree to look for birds' eggs.'

Sukhu almost fell for her sister's plan for she too felt tempted to go out into the forest with Dukhu—if not to steal birds' eggs, then at least climb trees, which she loved, and to gather wild flowers. So  she almost said, 'Let's go!' But then she thought of what her father had said and she replied, 'No, no, we mustn't go out. Remember what father has asked us to do? Let's sit out on the veranda and spin.' So Sukhu sat down to spin and as she sat spinning, the Wind came huffing and puffing and blew away her wad of cotton.

Sukhu ran after her cotton, but the Wind blew faster and faster and she could not keep pace with it. Exhausted, she burst into tears, and began to cry aloud when she heard the Wind say, 'Do not cry, Sukhu. Come with me to the Mother of Moon's palace and I will give you as much cotton as you need.'

Sukhu wiped her eyes and followed the Wind. Dukhu too followed behind saying, 'Wherever you go,

Sukhu, I shall always follow you.' So, the two sisters ran and ran following the Wind and on their way they met a Cow.

'Hamba! Hamba!' mooed the Cow. 'Don't run so fast, girls. My shed is covered with dirt and dung and it must be swept and washed clean. Will you clean my shed, please? I don't like giving milk in an unclean place.'

'I'll gladly clean your shed, Mother Cow,' said Sukhu

at once.

But Dukhu said haughtily, 'Insolent Cow! How dare you ask us to clean your filth? Fat chance! Don't you know, we're on our way to the Mother of Moon's palace?'

But Sukhu, disregarding her sister, at once fetched water from the well and then making a broom with a handful of dried palm leaves, she swept and washed the cowshed clean, while Dukhu stood grumbling, 'Nasty, nasty! This Cow has no sense at all! Why should we be asked to clean the cowshed? Let's not waste time, Sukhu.'

The Wind however, waited for Sukhu to finish her work and only when she had finished sweeping and washing the cowshed, did it begin to blow again, leading the girls to the Mother of Moon's palace. The two sisters ran and ran after the Wind and on their way they met a Tree.

'Where are you going, my pretty lassies?' cried the Tree. 'Don't run so fast. Wait a while and pull out the prickly nettles crowding at my feet, for they keep prickling and tingling me and I can't bend down to scratch my itching trunk!'

'I'll gladly do that for you, Sir!' said Sukhu with a nod of her head.

But Dukhu said haughtily, 'Brazen Tree! How dare you ask us to pull out the prickly nettles that grow at your feet? Don't you know, we're on our way to the Mother of Moon's palace?'

But Sukhu, disregarding her sister, bent down to pull out the prickly nettles, while Dukhu stood grumbling, 'Nasty, nasty! The Tree has no sense at all, making us stop on our way to get some cotton! Let's not tarry, Sukhu.'

The Wind however, waited for Sukhu to finish her work and only when she had finished, did it begin to blow again, leading Sukhu to the Mother of Moon's palace. And the two sisters ran and ran after the Wind and on their way they met a Horse.

'Don't run so fast, lassies. Stop for a while here and remove the bridle and the saddle from my back, please, for these are cutting into my flesh and hurting me, so that I can't bend down to eat grass.'

'I'll gladly take off your bridle and your saddle, Brother Horse,' said Sukhu, patting the Horse's handsome rump.

But Dukhu said haughtily, 'Impertinent Horse! Who do you think we are? The daughters of your groom? Don't you know, we're on our way to the Mother of Moon's palace?'

But Sukhu, disregarding her sister, at once took off the bridle and the saddle from the Horse's back, while Dukhu stood grumbling, 'Nasty, nasty! The Horse has no sense at all! Why should we care if the saddle and the bridle hurt the Horse's back? Let's not tarry, Sukhu.'

The Wind however, waited for Sukhu and only when she had removed the bridle and the saddle from the Horse's back and nursed its wounds, applying a poultice with a paste of healing neem leaves, did it began to blow again, leading Sukhu to the Mother of Moon's palace. And huffing and puffing it blew on and on and Sukhu and Dukhu ran on and on behind it, their little pigtails, tied with red ribbon bows, flying in the air, their colourful chintz skirts swollen with the wind like two gaily painted balloons.

Then at last, the Wind stopped and said to Sukhu, 'Do you see that palace there? That's where the Mother of Moon lives. Go in and she will give you all that you need.' Saying so, huffing and puffing the Wind blew away with a noise like this: *Woooooooosshh!*

Sukhu followed by Dukhu now entered the palace through a silver gate. They had never seen a house so beautiful before than the palace that was the dwelling of the Mother of Moon! Everything here shone with silver light. The trees outside the palace window danced in the silver light. The rooms inside the palace had a silver gleam. And the curtains and the rugs shone silvery bright. But there was something odd about this place for all the rooms were silent and empty. No one seemed to live in the palace except for a silver cat and a silver mouse with silver paws and silver eyes.

Quietly, on tiptoes Sukhu and Dukhu walked from room to room feeling rather scared. Suddenly, from behind a closed silver door there came a sweet voice, 'Sukhu, Sukhu, come in!'

Sukhu followed by Dukhu gently pushed open the silver door and lo and behold, there sat the Mother of Moon on a silver chair, radiating a silver glow. Her silver hair cascaded down from her silver head to the silver floor like a rippling silver stream. And her dress was made of silver threads and silver beads. She sat spinning at a silver wheel.

Sukhu bowed to the silver lady and touched her silver feet, saying, 'O, Mother of Moon, will you give me some cotton? The Wind has blown away my wad of cotton while I sat spinning on my veranda. And if I do not get back my cotton, I cannot spin while Father is away. And if I do not spin, we shall have nothing to eat.'

'Of course, of course, I'll give you your cotton and much more if you so desire. But before that, go and take a dip in my silver pond for you must be tired. Mind you, take only two dips. Twice, but not three times can you take a dip in my pond!'

'Can I take a dip in the silver pond too, Grandmother?' asked Dukhu without even bothering to greet the Mother of Moon.

'Indeed, indeed!' replied the silver lady. But she warned, 'Remember to take only two dips. Twice, but not three times can you take a dip in my pond!'

Sukhu and Dukhu ran out of the silver palace and through a winding silver path they came to the silver pond and plunged into the silver water to take a dip. When they emerged from the water, lo and behold, they found themselves changed into two dazzling damsels.

'You're looking gorgeous, Dukhu!' exclaimed Sukhu.

'You too are looking so beautiful!' exclaimed Dukhu.

Full of excitement, the two girls now took their second dip. And lo and behold, the weavers' girls were now changed into two pretty princesses, all dressed in silk and satin with gold jewels studded with diamonds, emeralds, rubies and sapphires adorning their slender arms and neck. The two girls now ran back to the palace to express their gratitude to the Mother of Moon. Sukhu at once touched her feet and asked for her blessings. But Dukhu stood in a corner showing off her ornaments, while the Mother of Moon said, 'My pretty princesses, you must be hungry! Go on to the next room for I want you to have a feast.'

Sukhu and Dukhu went into the next room and sitting down on silver chairs and at a silver table ate their fill. They had pulao made of the finest of fragrant basmati rice all garnished with currants and cashewnuts; they had bowls of golden dal cooked with coconut; they had curries flavoured with aromatic spices, and sweet rasgullas. Then they went back to the Mother of Moon to thank her for everything and bid her goodbye.

As the girls were about to leave, the Mother of Moon said to them, 'My pretty princesses, take home with you another gift.' She showed the two girls three caskets, each bigger than the next. 'Take one each but open them only when you reach home,' she said, offering the boxes to the delighted girls.

Sukhu took the smallest one, while Dukhu took the biggest and then they left. But on their way out,

Dukhu ran back to the silver pond saying, 'Come, Sukhu, this is a magic pond! Let's have another dip. Maybe we'll get many more jewels! Maybe we'll become even more beautiful!' Saying so, she took another plunge into the pond. Sukhu was tempted to follow her sister. 'Shall I go, shall I not?' she thought. But in the end she changed her mind, remembering what the Mother of Moon, who was so kind, had said.

And it was good that Sukhu did not fail to obey. For alas! Dukhu came out of the water with two horns on her head and a nose that was as long as an elephant's trunk! Sukhu could not believe what she saw. Dukhu burst into tears. Howling and crying she made her way home, but she did not forget her casket, which she held tightly to her chest.

As the two girls ran home, they met the Horse, the Tree and the Cow and each gave a gift to Sukhu for having helped them. The Horse gave Sukhu a young colt, a flying horse that could fly to any corner of the world. The Tree gave her a basket full of fruit made of gold and a sack full of gold coins. And the Cow gave her a young calf with udders that would never dry. And all of them said to her, 'Thank you, Sukhu, you're a good girl! Thank you for all the trouble you took in helping us.'

Sukhu too thanked them all for the wonderful gifts she had received and riding her flying horse, Sukhu and her sister, Dukhu, flew home.

When they reached home Dukhu ran and hid behind a tree, from where she called, 'We're home, Mother and Father! Look, what we've got!' The weaver and his wife had made themselves sick with anxiety, not knowing where the girls had gone. Now they were relieved to have their daughters back. Sukhu hugged her mother and showed her all her jewels and gifts. But Dukhu was nowhere to be seen. The weaver called out, 'Where is Dukhu? I've heard her voice, but why don't I see her?' And his wife too called, 'Why are you hiding behind the tree, Dukhu? Come here!'

Slowly Dukhu came out from behind the tree. When her father and mother saw her, they burst into tears. But soon they heard from Sukhu all that had passed and they chided Dukhu for failing to obey the Mother of Moon. 'You have yourself to thank for the trouble you're in!' they admonished. But Dukhu

 said, 'Mother and Father, do not worry! Let's see what's in this big casket. Perhaps there's a nice surprise in it for me and the old hag, the Mother of Moon, is going to make up for the way she's treated me!'

So saying she clicked the box open and as she did so, a young man sprang out from the box, saying, 'Dukhu, I'll be pleased to marry you.' The man too had horns on his head, exactly like Dukhu's, and—will you believe it oh my sweet children—he also had a nice long striped and hairy tail!

Sukhu too now opened her tiny casket. And as she clicked it open, a handsome prince came out of the box and said, 'Sukhu, I'll be pleased to marry you.'

The weaver and the weaver's wife were now in a fix. They did not know what to say or do. On the one hand they had suddenly come into wealth and on the other they were sorry for Dukhu. But Dukhu was happy to have found a man who was just like her.

And Sukhu was happy to have found a handsome prince who was as kind and loveable as she was, for the prince said to the weaver and the weaver's wife, 'Come and live with us in our palace, yonder there beyond the forest.' And to Dukhu he said, 'Since you've followed your sister everywhere, come and live with us in the palace with your man with a tail, but you shall have the palace wing in the backyard. There you can climb guava trees and mango trees and jamun trees all day long!' This made Dukhu's man quite happy, and he began to swish and wag his nice long striped and hairy tail!

Soon, the wedding day was fixed and Sukhu and Dukhu were married happily, Sukhu to the kind and lovable prince and Dukhu to her man with two horns and a tail.

Crazy Demons and Deadmen

The Barber and the
Mamdo Demon

Once upon a time, in a little village, there lived a barber. He was a very clever man. No one in his village could ever outwit him. And because he had great presence of mind, every villager—the fisherman, the cowherd, the boatman, the honey-seller and even the schoolmaster—came to him asking for his counsel whenever they found themselves in trouble. But it was not enough to be clever and give people good advice. The barber needed money to feed his family. This he did not have. He was so poor, he could hardly make both ends meet. Every morning he went from house to house solving people's problems and in the evening returned home empty-handed.

One evening, the barber returned home as usual without having earned even a rupee. Seeing this, his wife treated him to a long sermon: 'What shall I cook for our children? There is no rice in the kitchen. Would it not be better, husband dear, if you worked a little harder? All day long you do nothing but sit idle under the old banyan tree!'

The barber loved his wife. He did not like to see her sad and unhappy. But as he could do nothing about her complaints, he said to his wife, 'Times have changed, wife dear. Few men care for a shave from a roadside barber these days. I must leave home and go and look for some other work. And I shall come back only if I can bring home riches.'

So, next morning, as soon as the cock crowed cock-a-doodle-do, the barber left his home, taking with him in his bag only an old mirror, a broken comb, a razor, a few papayas to eat on the way and his pet parrot, Tia.

The barber tramped on and on. He crossed jade-green paddyfields, yellow mustard fields and blue-green ponds in which bloomed pink lotuses and in which swam ducks and geese and jet-black cormorants. He crossed sprawling fields of red barren earth on which crawled tiny red velvety mites. All day long the barber journeyed and at last, when the sun was about to set, he decided to rest for a while under the tall palmyra tree that stood in the distance at the edge of a forest, swaying its crown of long, bending leaves. The barber was hungry and thirsty, so he decided to eat his papayas sitting under the tree. But as darkness was falling fast and a strong howling wind had risen, he began to feel a little frightened.

As he came close to the tree, he saw to his horror that it was not a tree but a tall, lanky Mamdo Demon that inhabits the open fields of red barren earth. As tall as a palmyra tree, the demon stood upon his long, stick-thin legs which looked like two bamboo poles, with his skinny arms outspread. And as he stared down at the barber, the demon shook his huge head of shaggy hair that resembled the bending leaves of the palmyra tree. Making a shrieking sound and baring his enormous radish-like teeth, he had been flying through the air, making his way to a twelve demon's dance party deep in the forest. On seeing the barber from above, he had come down and stood waiting for him. 'Such a tiny man, what is he doing here?' the demon wondered. But glad he was indeed to see the barber, for he was hungry. And singing at the top of his nasal voice, '*Tat tai taha! Dhit tai taha! Tai dhit thai!*' the demon started to dance wildly.

The barber began to shake and shiver with fright but keeping his wits about him and mustering his courage, he too began to dance, keeping time with the demon and reciting at the top of his voice, '*Ta ta thai thai! Dhiki dhiki thai thai!*

'*Tat tai taha! Dhit tai taha! Tai dhit thai!*' The demon stamped his long feet as he danced and sang ever more loudly.

The barber was not going to let the demon outdo him. '*Ta ta thai thai! Dhik Dhik thai thai!*' he sang still louder.

The demon was surprised. Stopping his dance, he asked the barber, 'What makes you dance? What makes you so happy?'

'You tell me first! What
makes *you* dance?' the barber
snapped back boldly.

'No! You tell me!' the demon demanded.
And after a long argument, the demon
gave in and said, 'Ah, it's because I will feast
on you!'

The barber was horrified to hear this. But his mind
raced fast and he said quickly, 'How can you feast

on me? I have captured a dozen demons like you and they are all in my bag.'

The demon simply could not believe what he had heard. 'What is the man saying? A dozen demons in his bag? He must be lying,' he thought. So, throwing a challenge, the demon said, 'How can a tiny man like you capture giants like us? Let's have a contest of strength. Show me how strong you are!'

'No! You show me first how strong *you* are,' the barber said, even though he was very afraid.

'All right! I will show you how strong I am!' the demon replied. And picking up a huge boulder, he crushed it to dust with both his hands. 'See that?' he laughed frighteningly.

Now it was the barber's turn. What was he going to do? O, my children, don't forget that the barber was indeed a very clever man. So, he quietly took out a papaya from his bag and pressed it hard until the juice from the fruit oozed out. 'See that? I can take out juice even from a stone! Can you?'

The demon hummed and huffed and thought and at last said, 'But can you throw a stone into the sky

as high as I can?' Saying so, he
hurled a huge boulder in the air
that went flying like a ball up in
the sky, then came back and fell
with a thud on the ground.

'Ah! This is nothing compared to
what I can do,' the barber
asserted. 'Just you wait, I will
show you!' Saying so, he quietly
took out his pet parrot Tia
and threw it into the
air. Of course,
if flew off.
'See that? I
have thrown it so
far that it will not
come back!'

The demon blinked his eyes in complete astonishment. The barber laughed and said, 'Ah ha! So you see who is the stronger of the two?'

The demon nodded his head. The barber quickly added, 'You see, because I am stronger than you are, I have already captured you. You are in my bag!' Saying so, he quickly took out his mirror from his bag and held it up to the demon. 'Bend down a bit and look into this. Who is in here?' the barber asked, chuckling loudly.

The demon had never seen a mirror before in his life. He stooped low to inspect it and saw his own image in the looking-glass. He was horrified and he began to shake with fright. 'Why, yes! I'm in there! This man has captured me!' the dimwit demon thought.

And the clever barber, putting the mirror back into his bag said, 'And now, I have you in my bag.'

'What will you do with me now?' the demon asked meekly.

'I am a poor man and my wife and children are hungry.

I shall take you to my village and feast on you,' the barber said boldly.

The demon now began to tremble all over his skinny, long arms and all over his skinny, long legs and he begged and pleaded of the barber, 'O please, release me! I shall not feast on you, I promise!'

The barber quickly thought and pretending not to agree at first, he struck a deal. 'To get something, you must give something—that is fair, you know! What

will you give me, if I were to give you back your freedom?' the barber asked.

'I will give you anything that you want,' the demon promised at once. 'If you let me go, I shall reward you with enormous wealth!'

'Enormous wealth? What more do I need?' the barber thought. So he quickly agreed, 'All right, I shall release you, but only after you have carried me and the wealth you promise to my village home.'

To this the demon at once agreed. And as demons have special power, even if they are rather dimwitted, he at once produced enormous pots of gold coins, precious stones, laddus and grains, and together with the barber flew into the sky and made for the barber's village.

When the barber knocked at the door of his house, his wife unbolted it.

'Look there! Look, what I have got for you!' the barber exclaimed.

The barber's wife burst out laughing. 'Is this all you have brought home for us, husband dear? Now what are we going to do with a tall palmyra tree?' she asked, even though she was happy to see her husband come back home.

'No, no, this isn't a palmyra tree! Look carefully,' the barber said, and drawing his wife aside he told her all that had happened. The barber's wife was delighted as the demon now came and placed the pots full of goodies in her courtyard. But she certainly did not want a demon in the house for long. So she pleaded with her husband to quickly release him.

The barber also thought, 'Let me get rid of this simpleton Mando Demon before he finds out the truth!' So he quickly produced from his bag his mirror and showed the back of his looking-glass to the demon. The demon peered into the back of the mirror and gave an enormous sigh of relief at not finding his image in it. He now thought that he was at last free and with three long jumps he escaped to the far end of the red barren earth beyond the green paddy fields and the blue-green ponds in which bloomed pink lotuses and in which swam ducks and geese and jet-black cormorants.

The Brahma Demon's Marriage

A long time ago, there lived a poor man named Bhola brahman. In the good old days of his ancestors, the brahmans, or the village priests, had lived pretty comfortable lives, going from hut to hut offering prayers for the households and in return being handsomely rewarded with rice, milk and fruits that kept their wives quite content. But times had changed. There were more things to buy in the market now and Bhola brahaman's wife, Rudrakali, was simply not satisfied with her husband's paltry earnings. One day, when Bhola returned home from his round of prayers at the village huts with only one coconut, half a dozen bananas and rice and some ghee, which the richest man in the village had offered Bhola for his services, Rudrakali flew into a wild rage. 'Is this all you could bring home for me? We've enough coconuts and bananas growing in our fields! What about bringing home some money to buy new clothes? The potter's wife is lucky! Her husband gives her the money to buy soap and hair oil and new clothes. And all you bring home for me is a coconut and half a dozen bananas!' she fumed.

'It's your bad luck that you married me!' Bhola said nonchalantly. 'You can do nothing about it!'

'I can do nothing about it?' Rudrakali raved. 'I shall show you what I can do about it!' And saying so, she aimed the coconut at Bhola's head that was smooth and shiny and bald but for a few strands of hair that dangled at the back of his head. Then, pulling off the chaddar from his shoulders and flinging it on the floor and nearly taking off his dhoti, she lifted broom with both her hands and gave him a sound whacking.

Bhola was mortally afraid of his wife, especially when she got into a fit of rage. Even an angry bull was not half as dangerous as she was when annoyed, and like a little boy, he began to shiver and to shake all over his skinny legs and arms as his wife hollered and howled and beat him up thoroughly. He tried to duck every time Rudrakali came charging at him with her broom, but she was too swift for him and the broom landed on his head, his back, his arms and once— *chapak*—right on his face. In the frenzy of the moment, Bhola decided then and there to leave his wife and flee to another village far, far away from the reach of Rudrakali's broom and her vile tongue. So he managed somehow to slip on his wooden slippers, and picking up his chaddar and clutching at his dhoti, he ran for his dear life. Like a fierce hurricane, Rudrakali came yelling and yelping after him. 'O my good-for-nothing husband, don't you think you can run away from me!' she shrieked. 'I shall follow you to the end of the world to give you another thrashing!'

'Phoo!' cried Bhola brahman as he sprinted as fast as his heels could carry him and at last he reached a village that was five villages away from his own. Unable to keep up speed with her husband, Rudrakali returned to her hut, bellowing and bemoaning, 'O, poor me! How shall I live without a husband to beat up sometimes?'

But for Bhola brahman what a great relief it was to have escaped from Rudrakali! Praising the gods for their mercy, he now found himself a hut, where he alone was the monarch of his life. Now he didn't have to get up in the morning as soon as the cocks cried Cock-a-doodle-doo to do the dishes and to help out his wife with the household chores. He didn't have to cut up the vegetables for his wife to do the cooking. He didn't have to sweep and swab the floor, for Rudrakali easily tired cooking a pot of gruel rice and boiled potatoes, so that Bhola brahman had to do all these things for his wife's sake. And best of all, he didn't have to hear his wife nagging him all day long and all evening and through the night as well. If ever a mosquito bit Rudrakali on her back or her legs, she woke up Bhola right in the middle of the night and made him scratch and soothe her back and her legs, till she fell fast asleep and began to snore—*Phoor-phoor-phoo*!

At last Bhola had found perfect bliss—he had the freedom to do what he liked in his new home in the village that was five villages away from the one where Rudrakali lived. Most of the time, after offering prayers at the houses of the villagers, he stretched himself beneath the peepal tree and snored away, or he sat watching the crows cawing or the women going to the river ghats to bathe or fill up their pitchers.

But one day—it so often happens that good days are short, sweet and numbered—Bhola brahman fell seriously ill. As he didn't have a wife to nurse him— to be fair, Rudrakali did look after him in such times, giving him a day or two off from doing the dishes— he soon kicked the bucket. Poor Bhola! He had hoped to head straight for heaven after death, but whatever happened to him now? He found he had taken on a new form—that of a Brahma Demon—and so he wandered off to the far end of the village to live in a hole on the bole of a wood-apple tree that grew next to the burning ghat.

Climbing up the tree, his new residence, he wondered why he had been denied paradise—was he not the respected spirit of a priest? Sitting on his perch, it at last dawned upon him—it was because he had many a times stolen dates and mangoes from the offerings that the villagers had made to the gods and goddesses when he had been a priest. And a brahman who cheats and steals, instead of reaching heaven's gate after death must surely end up living on a tree as a Brahma Demon. At first Bhola was a little upset over this, but on second thoughts, he decided it was not such a bad thing to be a Brahma Demon! For now at last there was no chance whatsoever of Rudrakali ever finding out where he lived. He hoped that in the lives to follow he would never meet Rudrakali again. Was it not a shame for a man to be beaten up by his wife?

There was also another very good reason for the Brahma Demon to be happy in his arboreal abode. Surrounding his tree were several other trees—sal, coconut, peepal and banyan—that were all inhabited by a dozen pretnis, or female spirits, who paid him great attention. True, Bhola had been rather unlucky so far as women were concerned when he was a man. But now that he was a Brahma Demon, overnight he had become a hot favourite with a bevy of pretnis, who did their best to woo him by singing and dancing through the night and by showering endless affection on him, and by throwing fragrant blossoms at him whenever he happened to pass by their trees. If ever he looked up at them they giggled and called him in the sweetest of nasal voices. The Brahma Demon now didn't even have to bother about his meals. Every pretni brought him food and pampered him, for each hoped to marry him some day, as matrimony with a Brahma Demon was considered to be a blessing indeed among spirits.

One evening, soon after sunset, the Brahma Demon came out of his tree hole, and had clambered down the tree trunk to take a walk in the paddy-fields, when he heard two pretnis quarrel.

'I want to marry the Brahma Demon! There is no greater honour than to be the wife of a spirit of a respected priest!' said one.

And the other retorted, 'Have you ever seen the shadow of your face in the lake? You are the ugliest pretni I've ever seen! No, no, you won't make a good wife to him. You're too dark and thin like a bamboo pole for the Brahma Demon to like you!'

The Brahma Demon's heart sank at the thought of a wife! With a rude shock he remembered Rudrakali and her sharp tongue that was like the sharp thorn of the ber bush. At once he made up his mind never to marry again. 'I'm fine this way! Why get into trouble again with a marriage?' he thought. Quickly, he leaped up a tree and then jumping on to another and then another, he fled from the scene. But the two pretnis followed him and chased him till dawn began to break in the eastern sky, and both the pretnis and the Brahma Demon had to retire to their respective trees for the day.

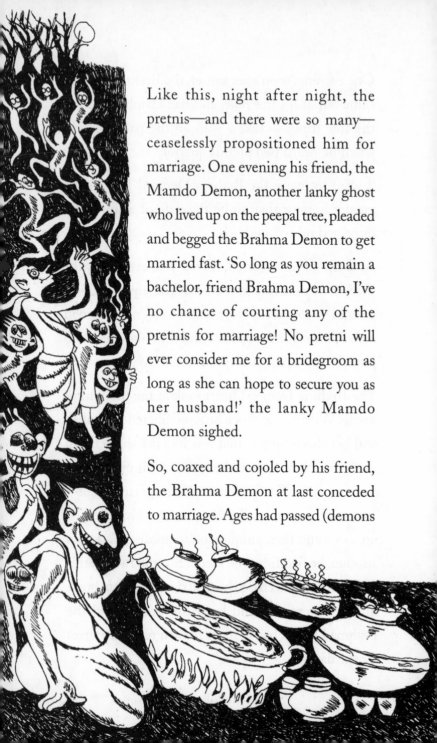

Like this, night after night, the pretnis—and there were so many—ceaselessly propositioned him for marriage. One evening his friend, the Mamdo Demon, another lanky ghost who lived up on the peepal tree, pleaded and begged the Brahma Demon to get married fast. 'So long as you remain a bachelor, friend Brahma Demon, I've no chance of courting any of the pretnis for marriage! No pretni will ever consider me for a bridegroom as long as she can hope to secure you as her husband!' the lanky Mamdo Demon sighed.

So, coaxed and cojoled by his friend, the Brahma Demon at last conceded to marriage. Ages had passed (demons

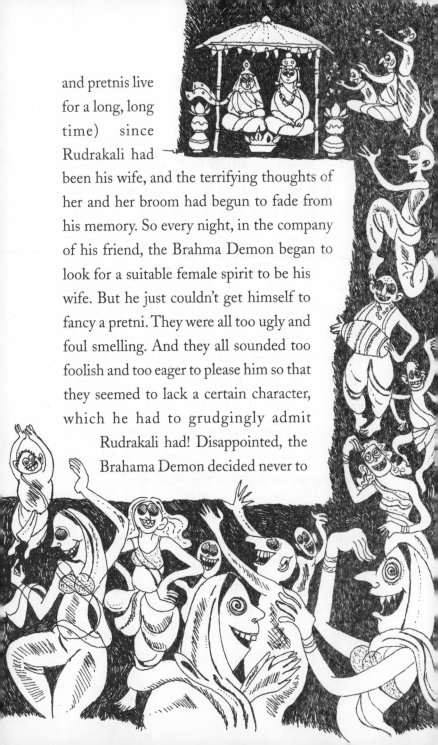

and pretnis live
for a long, long
time) since
Rudrakali had
been his wife, and the terrifying thoughts of
her and her broom had begun to fade from
his memory. So every night, in the company
of his friend, the Brahma Demon began to
look for a suitable female spirit to be his
wife. But he just couldn't get himself to
fancy a pretni. They were all too ugly and
foul smelling. And they all sounded too
foolish and too eager to please him so that
they seemed to lack a certain character,
which he had to grudgingly admit
Rudrakali had! Disappointed, the
Brahama Demon decided never to

tie the nuptial knot again, till, one night, his friend brought him great news.

'A new pretni has recently come to live in the locality and she doesn't smell too foul; besides, everyone agrees that she is a great beauty with large round red eyes and a rare dark-green countenance,' the Mamdo Demon said. Hearing this, the Brahma Demon was pleased. At last the right pretni bride was found, and he at once set about making preparations for the wedding feast. Pots and pots of dead rats and dried bats, boiled snails and roasted cockroaches, grilled worms and fried lizards were ordered for the feast. Even though the pretnis who were rejected by the Brahma Demon were all heartbroken, there was much merry-making and singing and dancing and yelling and thumping and screaming on the night of the wedding.

Finally, the feasting was over and the guests were all gone and the Brahma Demon decided to take a look at last at his bride's face in the bright moonlight. She was sitting coyly, dressed in a bride's fineries with her head lowered and covered with the end of her sari which was studded with a thousand fireflies that looked like so many glittering diamonds! He had only heard from his friend, the Mamdo Demon, about her ravishing beauty—her red round eyes and dark-green countenance. Now at last he drew his pretni bride to his bosom to whisper sweet nothings into her ears as he slowly took off her veil. But oh horror! With a loud scream, the Brahma Demon fell off from his tree, then quickly got upon his feet and raced down the meadow at full speed. At his heel followed the pretni, swift like a whirlwind. She was none other than the spirit of Rudrakali!

'I've got you! I've got you again, my good-for-nothing husband!' Rudrakali shrieked as she went after the Brahma Demon. 'Stop! Stop!'

'I shall not stop!' shouted the Brahma Demon. 'But tell me Rudrakali, how on earth did you find me?'

The pretni giggled and replied, 'After you fled from me, no one was willing to marry me. Heartbroken I passed away within a month. Since then, I've been looking for you in every bush and every tree, for I had heard that you'd become a Brahma Demon. And just the other day a pretni told me that you lived up there on the wood-apple tree, next to the burning ghat. And that you were going to take a wife. I wasted no time . . .' Saying so, she was almost about to grab at the few strands of hair that dangled at the back of the Brahma Demon's bald head, when *plop*, he dived into a nearby pond and with the special powers of a Brahma Demon, he quickly emerged as a frog—the only creature that Rudrakali was afraid of.

'Shoo! Shoo!' Rudrakali cried, quickly clambering up a tree. And never again did she venture near the pond. But people say they have sometimes seen and heard, in the deep dark night, a pretni bride, broom in hand, wailing for her demon husband.

Speaking Animals

Uncle Jackal and His Two Nephew Otters

A jackal was passing by when he heard two otters quarrelling among themselves on the riverbank.

'Cut it into equal halves? No, never! I deserve a wee bit more than you!' claimed one with a swish of his stout tail.

And the other, flaring up his thick whiskers, argued, 'I deserve a wee bit more than you!'

The otters argued and squeaked and grunted and almost came to blows. Now, what was the dispute over? The jackal wondered if the two could be fighting over a plate of something to eat, when—Hukka Hua! He could hardly believe his ears!—he suddenly heard the word 'fish'. At once lifting up his muzzle and expanding his nostrils, he sniffed the air hard. Sure enough, there was a tang of fish in the air! The jackal was hungry and the scent of fish made his mouth water. He loved fish so much that he sometimes wondered if, in his previous birth, he had been a fishing bird! But now that he was a jackal, he could hardly catch a fish. How many months was it that he hadn't had a dish of fish for lunch? Besides, he had had no breakfast and no lunch the whole day, because he had been too lazy to hunt or scavenge for a meal. Now his stomach was crying out to him for a dish of something yummy, yummy. Swallowing his

saliva, the jackal quickly shot through the undergrowth to the riverbank where the two otters were arguing. 'I, Hondu the otter, have chased the fish in the river and brought it to the riverbank and only then could you, Bhondu, catch it!' said one.

And the other said, 'I, Bhondu the otter, have actually caught the fish! Had I not, you, Hondu, would have to go hungry.'

'I worked harder than you, driving the fish against the water current to the riverbank for you to catch it! I deserve more!' asserted Hondu.

'No, I deserve more than you!' reasserted Bhondu. 'I'm the hunter!'

'What good is an otter, if he cannot even catch a fish?' mocked Hondu.

'And what good is an otter, if he cannot even swim after a fish?' sneered Bhondu.

Like this, the two otters teased one another mercilessly and each said they deserved a wee bit more than the other of the fish they had caught.

The jackal, hiding behind a jackfruit tree, overheard all this. And he quickly thought of a plan. Calling out loudly 'Hukka hua! Hukka hua!' he approached Hondu and Bhondu and asked in the friendliest of voices, 'Hey, nephews! What is this brawl over? Tut, tut! I'm sorry to see my sweet nephews fighting over a fish, when you two should actually be playing and having fun in the river like true otters! Could your Uncle Jackal help you two to settle your dispute?'

The otters were delighted to hear a jackal addressing himself as their uncle and calling them most tenderly 'his nephews'. Gladly they accepted their uncle's offer of help to mediate and to judge as to who actually deserved a wee bit more of the fish.

'Should you abide by my judgement, I shall be only too pleased to decide your case,' the wily jackal quickly said, looking lovingly at each of the otters, so that both Hondu and Bhondu thought that dear Uncle Jackal would surely take his side.

'We'll certainly abide by your judgement, Uncle!' the otters promised. And the cunning jackal, crying 'Hukka hua! Hukka hua!' with utmost delighted, at once took Hondu to a corner and asked him to explain as to why he thought he deserved a wee bit more than Bhondu.

'I, Hondu the otter, have worked the hardest, driving the fish against the water current to the riverbank for Bhondu to catch it! Surely, I deserve more!' declared Hondu. And Uncle Jackal nodding his head said, 'Indeed, indeed, my nephew Hondu! You've worked hard swimming deep into the midstream, braving the dangers of the river, facing the turtle and the crocodile and the water-snake and undaunted you've chased the fish to the riverbank for Bhondu to catch it. Indeed, you've worked very hard!'

Hondu was delighted. 'Surely Uncle will give me a bigger piece of fish!' he thought as he returned to the riverbank where Bhondu stood guarding the fish and waiting anxiously for them.

Now, casting sidelong glances at the fish, Uncle Jackal

at once took Bhondu aside, leaving Hondu to guard the fish. He asked Bhondu to explain as to why he thought he deserved a wee bit more than Hondu. And Bhondu replied, 'I, Bhondu the otter, have actually caught the fish! Had I not, Hondu would have to go hungry.'

'Indeed, indeed, my nephew, Bhondu! You've done a very commendable job by catching a fish on the riverbank!' said the hungry jackal with a short laugh. 'It is you, Bhondu, who've actually caught the fish and how can I deny that you've been so brave!'

Bhondu was delighted. 'Surely, Uncle will give me a bigger piece of fish!' he thought as he returned to the riverbank where Hondu stood waiting anxiously for them and keeping an eye on the fish.

The Jackal now made Hondu and Bhondu sit down, quietly telling them he would shortly give his judgement. With bated breath the two otters waited for their Uncle to speak. But without a word, the Jackal sliced the fish into two unequal halves—the piece with the tail being much bigger than the piece with the head. The two otters were delighted. And Hondu thought that he would surely be rewarded with the

larger share. And Bhondu thought that he would surely be rewarded with the larger share. But oh, horror of horrors! Far from what the two otters were hoping to hear, Uncle Jackal was now stammering and stuttering, 'Err—I am sorry! I'm very, very sorry! Err—I should have divided the fish into two equal halves, for both of you have worked equally hard. Err—both of you deserve an equal share!'

And now, to make the two pieces equal, Uncle Jackal coolly bit off a large chunk of fish from the piece that was bigger, so that now, only the tail remained.

Then, holding up the two pieces of fish to his nose and examining them, he stammered and stuttered again, 'Err—a mistake! A mistake again, my nephews! Err—I've again made a horrible mistake. Both of you deserve an equal share! But look at this! The piece with the head is now much, much larger than the other piece! I shall have to do something about it at once!' And saying so, he once again coolly bit off a large chunk of fish from the piece that was larger, so that now only the head remained. And then, with a loud guffaw, he asked, 'Haven't I made a very fair judgement?'

At last Hondu and Bhondu understood what the jackal had been up to so long. But it was too late. For

now, only the head and the tail remained, which the jackal threw at the otters, saying, 'I do hope you'll abide by my judgement!' And having eaten up the best succulent middle part, Uncle Jackal took leave of his two nephews and shot through the undergrowth, crying 'Hukka hua! Hukka Hua!'

'We've been utter fools, fighting among ourselves!' exclaimed Hondu, his thick whiskers drooping.

'And when fools fight, rogues and rascals win the fight!' declared Bhondu, wagging his tail meekly.

Then, sharing the head and the tail of the fish equally between themselves, Hondu and Bhondu linked paws and sliding down the riverbank in true otter style, fell with a loud splash into the river, laughing and giggling.

The Non-violent Snake

By the blue-green village pond, in which swam golden-brown ducks, was the best green rolling field of golden grain that danced in the sweetest of breezes. In this best green rolling field in which danced golden grain in the sweetest of breezes, there lived a dour-faced, sour-tempered, sulky-bulky slithering snake named Phos-phos. Everyone in the village—the potter, the weaver, the honey-seller, the milkmaid, the kite-maker, the fisherman, the farmer and all the womenfolk and children—kept their distance from him and shunned him because of the snake's habit of rushing at people and biting whoever happened to cross his way.

'A wily, vile, wicked snake he is!' the farmer said.

'Ugh! Look at his cold, cruel eyes!' the potter exclaimed.

'Wait till I catch him one day and give him a good thrashing,' the cowherd boy said.

And as dusk began to fall, all the village women would cry out to their children, 'Come back home! Don't loiter in the fields for Phos-phos may be hiding in the grass!'

Even the cow, the cock and the pig disliked the snake. 'Beware of the snake in the grass—it bites!' they warned.

In fact, no one in the village ever tried to make friends with Phos-phos, for they were all afraid of him. Whenever they saw him coming through the grass, sliding towards them, even when he had a smile upon his dour face, they jumped up and fled. And Phos-phos would call out in vain, 'Oh, ho! Fisherman! Oh, ho! Farmer! Oh, ho! Boys! Wait for me! Come, let's have a chat! I want to be your friend!' But there were no takers for the offer of the snake's friendship.

Phos-phos was very unhappy. 'It's not nice to have no friends! No one likes me! Is it my looks? Yes, I'm not handsome as the ducks or the big fat cows! I am

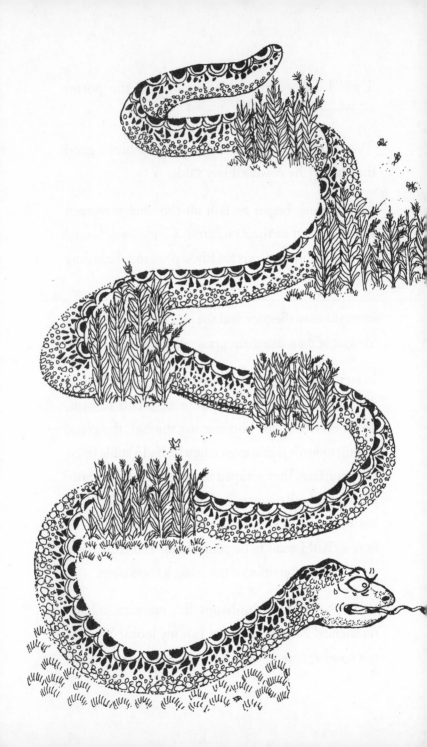

plain and have no limbs to walk! But what of that? It is Brahma, the Creator, who has made me so. But how I wish I could make friends with the village folk,' Phos-phos thought and sighed to himself.

One day, he decided to go and see the village priest and seek his advice. Winding his way through the green grass, he arrived at the village temple. 'Oh, ho! Holy man! Oh, ho! Temple priest! Can you tell me why no one wants me as a friend? Am I not good-looking? Am I not handsome?'

The holy man, who was sitting in deep meditation counting his beads, slowly opened his eyes and smiled and said, 'Whoever says Phos-phos is not handsome?

Most certainly you're good-looking! The sinuous movement of your supple body and the shine and pattern of your skin makes you most beautiful! The only problem is your bite!'

Flattered by the praises of the holy man, Phos-phos sat himself in a coil, swaying his hood in assent to what the holy man said. He thought, 'Yes, I must admit, there's nothing I like more than a good bite. Yes, I do love it!'

Then the holy man laughed and advised, 'Listen, my dear friend Phos-phos, promise me you will give up biting!'

Phos-Phos was delighted for the holy man had called him 'my dear friend', so he promised never to bite again. He returned home to the best green rolling field of golden grain that danced in the sweetest of breezes and going into his hole, he decided never to bite again. Since that day, he began to lead a non-violent life.

Soon word got round the village that Phos-phos had given up biting. The village folk—the honey-seller, the farmer, the kite-maker, the potter, the weaver, the fisherman and all the womenfolk and the children—heaved a sigh of relief.

'Ah, the wily, vile, wicked snake has given up biting, I hear,' the farmer laughed.

'We're safe at last in the green rolling field for there lives a harmless, non-violent snake!' cried the cowherd boy.

And as dusk descended upon the village, the womenfolk no longer worried about their children even when they played right under the snake's nose, for Phos-phos now sat in a coil flashing a smile at every passerby.

But poor Phos-phos! He had to soon learn the ways of the world. Ever since the time he gave up biting, he found that the villagers no longer feared him, and instead teased him mercilessly. The children even pelted stones at him and dragged him by his tail. 'Oouuchch! Oouuchch! Put me down! Put me down!' Phos-phos would cry out as the children lifted him up by his tail, twirled and whirled him in the air and threw him with a thud on a sharp-edged rock. Battered and bruised, he sat weeping while the village folk gave him a kick saying, 'Ah! It's a non-violent snake! It's a harmless snake that doesn't bite!'

One day, as the snake sat groaning and moaning by

the roadside, the village priest happened to pass by. He stopped to have a word with his disciple. The snake bowed before the holy man and said, 'Guru, I promised you to give up biting and I've kept my promise. Even when people kick me

and tease me, and beat me with sticks, I do not bite. But look, this is what I get in return for being a non-violent snake,' Phos-phos said displaying his wounds.

The holy man at once nursed the hurt snake and said, 'O my friend Phos-phos, don't be such a fool! I had asked you to give up biting, but did I ever ask you not to hiss at people and frighten them and chase them away when they come to harm you? Do not indulge in violence. Do not harm others. But learn as well to protect yourself when someone hurts you!'

At last, the dour-faced, sour-tempered, sulky-bulky snake understood what the holy man had said. Thanking the village priest and swaying his hood, he danced his way back into the best green rolling field of golden grain that swayed in the sweetest of breezes.

Just-so Stories

The Ghost of a Shepherd

A shepherd thought as he took his sheep to graze, 'My sheep are tired of eating grass every day. Why not go up that tamarind tree and fetch some fresh leaves for my sheep?' So, with an axe in hand, he climbed up the tree and sitting on the branch with the heaviest foliage, he began to hack at it. Chop, chop, chop, he went with his axe. 'Bah! My sheep will have a feast of tamarind leaves this morning!' he said to himself.

'Aieyo! Come down! Come down!' shouted a holy man, who happened to pass that way. 'You're cutting the very branch you're sitting on!'

'Why should I come down?' protested the shepherd, feeling rather annoyed for being told to come down when he was busy at work. 'I'm here atop the tree to get some fresh leaves for my sheep!' he called back.

'If you don't come down at once, you will fall along with the branch that you're chopping, you fool!' warned the holy man.

'No, I don't believe you!' shouted back the shepherd. 'How do you know I'll fall?'

The holy man couldn't help laughing. He realized that the shepherd was rather thick in the head. So he kindly explained to him, 'You see, you are hacking at the very branch you're sitting on. When the branch comes crashing down to the ground, you too will come down with a thud!'

'No! How can that be?' cried the shepherd. 'I don't quite understand what you're saying.'

'Well, well!' said the holy man with a smile, 'Let me explain to you with a practical example!'

The shepherd was glad. 'Explain to me with a practical example this so very incomprehensible thing, holy man!' he said.

So to give a practical example, the holy man instructed

the shepherd, 'Now go and sit on another branch. Then, take off your shirt and hang it on the branch that you're cutting.'

Like an obedient schoolboy the shepherd did what he was told to do. Then the holy man said, 'That's good, villager! Now, sitting on this branch, cut the branch on which you've hung your garment.' The shepherd again did what he was asked to do and the branch with the shepherd's shirt fell to the earth.

The shepherd was now greatly impressed. At once he came down the tree and fell at the holy man's feet. 'Swami, you know a lot! You're great!'

The holy man laughed and was about to walk away, pleased that he had saved a fellow villager from breaking a few bones, if not from death. But the shepherd would just not let the holy man go away. 'You're wise, Swami! You know so much! You're the most enlightened man I have ever met. Now tell me, when am I going to die?' he asked.

The holy man was taken aback. 'How shall I know about your death, foolish man? We mortals can never predict these things!'

But the shepherd insisted, 'O Swami, don't be so humble! I'm sure you know everything! Or else, how could you tell me that the branch I was cutting would fall! Do tell me Swami, when am 1 going to die— and I shall give you a sheep.'

The holy man was visibly annoyed and just to get rid of the shepherd said with a guffaw, 'You shall die when you feel hungry and your tongue feels parched and you sight the new moon.' Saying so, he hurried past the shepherd.

Since then, morning and night, as he tended his sheep or as he lay in bed, the shepherd thought of what the holy man had predicted. Months passed. The seasons rolled by. And years followed years. Then, one night, when the shepherd's wife was away, for she had gone to her mother's home, the shepherd woke up feeling hungry and thirsty. With a start, he sat up on his bed and from the window of his hut, he sighted the new moon. 'O goodness me! Tonight is the end of me! My time's up!' he sighed as he fell back in his bed and lay stiff and straight like a dead man. 'I'm going to die. I feel hungry and my throat feels parched and there is a new moon in the sky! I must not move. I must not talk,' the shepherd thought.

Not once did it occur to him that he was hungry because he had gone to bed on an empty stomach as his wife was away and he had been too lazy to cook.

Instead, all night long he lay motionless like dead wood.

The next morning, when the shepherd's wife returned home, she found her husband lying in bed, stiff and straight with his eyes shut. 'Are you unwell, my husband?' she asked anxiously.

The shepherd did not reply.

'Are you not going to get up today?'

There was no answer.

'Why don't you talk, my husband?' asked the wife tickling the man.

Still, there was no movement. No answer.

'Aieyo! Aieyo! Amma!' the wife yowled and howled and burst into loud sobs. 'My husband is dead! He doesn't talk! He doesn't move! He doesn't open his eyes!' She ran out of the house, her hair loose and her sari slipping off her shoulder, wailing and screaming to announce to the villagers that her husband had died while she was in her mother's house.

Hearing the bad news the villagers at once rushed to the shepherd's house to mourn. But at first, just to make sure that he was dead, they poked him and prodded him and pinched him and slapped his cheeks and tickled him under his arms and his feet. Yet the shepherd lay still—even though he wanted to giggle when he was tickled—and held his breath thinking, 'No, no, I must not tell them I'm not dead yet, for I'm going to die any moment. I must not move. I must not talk. I must lie still with my eyes shut for it's time for me to die as I feel hungry and my throat feels parched, and last night there was a new moon in the sky!'

The villagers found that the shepherd did not respond, so they cried, 'The shepherd is dead! He was a good shepherd, though bit of a fool!'

After the villagers had cried and mourned for the shepherd, taking him to be dead, they took off his clothes and wrapped him in a new cloth and carried him to the burial ground. There, after some more crying and mourning, they dug up a grave and buried him in the earth and left for the river to wash their hands, while in the dark of the night the jackals howled Hua! Hua! Hukka-hua!

Now, lying in his grave, unable to breathe, and hearing the jackals cry, a chill came over the shepherd. With all his might he kicked off the earth with his legs and thrashed his hands about and pushed away the soil that covered him. Then, getting up on his two feet, he raced after the villagers, crying, 'Hey, villagers! Don't you go away leaving me behind! Wait for me!'

When the villagers heard the shepherd, whom they had just buried, call out to them, they at once took to their heels and fled. While they sprinted at full speed, they took a quick look behind. Goodness gracious!

The shepherd was coming after them, crying and yelling, and he didn't have a single piece of cloth on him! He was all covered in mud and earth and dust and dirt.

'Amma! The shepherd's ghost is coming after us!' the villagers screamed as they all ran into their huts and tightly bolted their doors from inside. The shepherd was in a fix. What was he to do now? Who would now believe that he was not dead but had been only waiting to die, for had not the holy man predicted his death? Wondering how he could convince his wife that he was not yet a spirit, he walked over to her hut and knocked, calling out to his wife, 'Wife, wife, open the door. Let me in!'

When the shepherd's wife heard the voice of her husband calling out to her, she was petrified. Then, picking up courage, she slowly walked to the entrance on her wobbly legs and through a slit in the door saw her husband standing outside, stark naked and covered in mud and earth and dirt and dust. With teeth chattering, she implored, 'O my dear, departed husband, please go away to the nether world in peace. I shall offer a coconut at your grave and pray for the peace of your soul.'

In vain did the shepherd try to explain that he was not a ghost. The wife was too frightened to hear him out and she continued to plead, 'Please, please, dear departed husband, leave me alone in peace. Go away from my hut! Besides, it's not proper for a man, not even if he is a ghost, to go about without a piece of cloth to cover his shame!'

The shepherd had not thought of this! With a shock he realized that his wife indeed had a point. Perhaps no one minded if a man went about in public without an upper garment, but without a dhoti or a lungi on? No, no, that was far from being acceptable. Embarrassed, he ran into the forest of tamarind trees, wild date-palms and ber bushes that grew at the edge of the village and there he stayed all day, venturing out into the village only under the cover of darkness to look for something to eat. And if ever a villager came face to face with the naked shepherd, he jumped up and fled at once, screaming and crying, 'The shepherd's ghost is haunting our village!'

Soon, every villager rushed indoors and bolted his or her door, while the poor shepherd went in vain from house to house in the dark night, knocking at every door. No one ever did let him in—not even his wife. When he went to her hut and begged her to open the door, she simply refused to let a ghost in.

Like this, nights passed and the shepherd could no longer bear the rumblings of hunger in his stomach. Desperately he thought of a way to get out of the situation. And at last he had a brainwave! He decided to go to the dhobi ghat one morning and get some clothes to wear. Then he could go to the village in the daytime and tell the villagers that after all, he was not a spirit and that he had not died at all. So, one morning, before sunrise, he reached the washerman's place. Just then a policeman came riding with his dirty clothes to get them washed. The washerman too arrived just then. So quickly, to hide his shame, the shepherd plunged into the ubba, the vat in which the dirty clothes were boiled.

The policeman came and handed over his clothes to the washerman and the washerman took them and went to the vat to put them in for washing. And just as he did so he caught sight of the naked shepherd in his vat and with a loud scream he ran for his life hollering, 'The shepherd's ghost is in the vat!'

'Coward!' cursed the policeman. 'There's no such thing as a dirty, unwashed ghost that needs laundering! If you cannot put my clothes in the vat for a wash, I will!' He approached the vat with his dhoti and shirt. And as he put his clothes in, he took a quick peep in. He too saw the shepherd sitting in the vat with ashes and dirt smeared all over his body. Forgetting that he was a brave policeman, he sprang up like a Jack-in-the-box and with a loud shriek took to his heels. 'Aieyo! Aieyo! The shepherd's ghost is in the vat!' he cried as he ran. When the villagers saw the policeman fleeing, they too threw away their brooms and buckets, pots and pans and whatever they held in their hands and ran indoors and bolted their doors.

'Amma, what shall I do now? I've got to do something, or this is truly going to be the end of me,' the shepherd thought stroking his belly, and almost in tears. He was now so very hungry that he was no longer ashamed of coming out of the vat without a stitch on in broad daylight. But lying there he found the policeman's dhoti inside the vat and wrapped it around his waist. Boldly he marched to the village and knocked at his wife's door. 'Wife, wife, I've got a dhoti on, come and see!' he cried.

Hearing this, the shepherd's wife peeped out of her window, and when she saw her husband dressed like a man, she realized that he was not a ghost. She

quickly took him in and washed off the mud and the earth and the dirt and dust that covered his body and gave him clean clothes to wear. Then, she cooked for him and fed him hot steaming idlis and sent him to bed. But before he went off to take a nap, she asked him to tell her what had happened. The shepherd told her the truth and his wife laughed.

'It serves you right dear husband!' she said. 'Never should you blindly believe in anything anyone says. Believe in things as and when they happen!'

'Amma! My wife is such a clever woman! She is cleverer than the holy man! From now onwards, I shall only listen to my wife!' the shepherd thought and turning around, he began to snore—*Ghaaaaaar! Ghaaaaaar! Ghaaaaaar!*

The Valiant Potter

L ong, long ago, there lived a potter and his wife
in a little hamlet that nestled close to a forest at
the foot of the blue-green hills. The potter was poor
but he was quite content making pots of many shapes
and sizes and earthen lamps and toy figurines by
moulding the clay on his wheel and then drying and
glazing them over a little furnace. The potter's wife
was also happy going to the market everyday to sell
the earthenware her husband made, stacked on the
back of their donkey, named Tiger. And the donkey
too was happy working for the kind-hearted potter
and his wife. But one day, when after sunset the
donkey, which had gone for a walk in the forest in
the afternoon, did not return home, the potter and
his wife were grieved thinking that something terrible

had happened to it. The potter did not have the money to buy another donkey. And when the sun had set and it was dark and the donkey did not return home, the wife began to howl and wail, 'O my dear Tiger! What has become of you, my Tiger? A real tiger must have eaten you up in the forest! Now who will carry our earthenware to the market?' And between sobs and tears, she told the potter to go in search of the donkey in the thick forest, in the dark of the night.

In the thick, dark forest there lived a real tiger. This tiger was ferocious and ill-tempered, so that the poor potter shook with fright at the thought of having to go into the forest alone. And to drown his nervousness, he took a couple of extra glasses of toddy before he set off. Then, walking on wobbly legs and swaying from left to right and right to left and again from left to right and right to left all the way, the potter reached the forest. Just as he walked into the forest, the real tiger that was ferocious and ill-tempered, came down the road licking his lips, having had a hearty meal of deer meat. He had made a kill—an old Sambar deer that could not run very fast—after weeks, and so he was in a jolly good mood and he sang at the top of his growling, ear-splitting voice, his favourite song:

> Tasty tasty meat
> Crunchy munchy bones
> There is nothing that I love more than
> Tasty tasty meat
> And crunchy munchy bones.

The couple of extra glasses of toddy that the potter had drunk had gone straight to his head and it made him feel brave and bold and very, very imaginative. In the thick dark night, hearing the tiger sing in his growling, ear-splitting voice, he mistook it to be the braying of his donkey. At once running up to the tiger and seizing him by the tail, he began to beat him, box his ears, punch his nose, and rain blows on his beautiful golden back striped with black, for the potter had truly worked himself into a fit of proper rage. 'You braying brat of a donkey!' cried the potter. 'Your mother, my wife, has been crying for you and you have been sitting in the forest singing songs! Ha, think you're a tiger? Your name may be Tiger, but phoo, phoo that doesn't mean you're one. You're a donkey! Come home at once! Or I'll break every bone in your body.' Saying so, the potter leaped onto the tiger's back and giving it a tug by its tail forced it to walk on.

Never in his life had the tiger been so ill-treated. As a matter of fact, he had noticed men kept their distance from him and were generally in awe of him. But this man dared to call him, a tiger, the king of the forest, a lowly donkey! And on top of that he had beaten him up so badly! The tiger did not know what to make of it all, and feeling quite frightened, he went along meekly to the potter's house as he was commanded. When they reached the hut— the wife was fast asleep, having cried herself to sleep—the potter got down and hurling more abuses,

tied up the tiger's fore feet with a rope and tethered him to a post in his backyard.

Next morning, while the potter was still in bed, his wife got up and rubbing her sleepy swollen eyes, walked into the backyard. Then she got the shock of her life. Seeing the tiger tied to the post, she went running to wake up her husband. 'Such is your love for me, dear husband, that risking your life, you've brought home a real tiger for me!' she exclaimed with great joy and pride. Then, before the stunned potter could say a word, she ran out of her house to tell the villagers that her husband had brought home a tiger and tied it to a post. And soon, this extraordinary news spread far, far, far, from village to village, till it finally reached the ears of the young prince, who was the commander-in-chief of his father, the raja of Tamrapani's ten-thousand strong army.

Now, a war was about to break out between the kingdom of Tamrapani and the neighbouring state of Pappanadu, whose king being a belligerent man had amassed a huge army at the borders. But the young prince, the commander-in-chief, did not fancy going to war. He preferred to sing and dream and read poetry or plays, or play with his little sister, the young princess, in their enchanting garden. So, when he heard of the potter who had brought home a tiger, the most fearsome beast that everyone feared, he ran to his father and entreated him to make the potter the commander-in-chief of his army. The raja too was impressed with the potter and readily agreed. He called for the potter and made him the commander-in-chief of his army and honoured him with the title The Valiant Chattee-maker of Tamrapani. He also gave him a tall and handsome steed, a spirited charger to ride and put ten-thousand men at his command, saying, 'You who can keep a tiger in your backyard like one keeps pigs and chicken, O valiant chattee-maker, you shall surely put to flight our enemy!'

Now the potter was in a complete fix. He simply did not know what to do. Far from being able to lead an army, he couldn't even ride a horse and a war horse at that. He fretted and worried as the day fixed for the battle drew near. Then, his wife, who by now had understood the difficult position she had got her husband into, had a bright idea. 'Husband, why don't you take some riding lessons? Ask the raja to send you home the charger and try mounting it—at least learn to sit on the saddle before the war begins,' she advised.

To this, the potter at once agreed and the raja readily sent him home the charger, powerful, magnificent and richly caparisoned, so that he could get used to his horse and the horse to a valiant rider.

When the horse arrived, the potter was frightened to death at the thought of having to get upon its back, even though his wife did her best to keep up his spirit. He was sure he would make a fool of himself trying to ride the horse. Nevertheless, coaxed by his wife into giving it a try, he did make several attempts in a day to sit upon the horse.

'The saddle is so high up!' lamented the potter, looking up at it.

'Not so high if you give one great jump,' said his wife encouragingly.

'Sure, I can jump high, but this dhoti keeps flying up covering my eyes so that I do not know which way to turn,' said the potter thoughtfully.

'No, no, don't face the tail while you jump, face the head,' advised his wife.

And as he jumped, he cried, 'Wife, wife, where do I put my foot?'

'The right one goes into the right stirrup, the left one goes into the left,' cried out his wife.

The potter jumped but he fell down with a thud.

For seven days and seven nights, the potter tried to mount the horse with the help of his wife. But every time he did so, he fell off it. Sometimes his dhoti got caught in the stirrup and nearly came off. Sometimes he found himself sitting facing the tail of the horse. And sometimes, he jumped so high that taking a somersault he came down right on the other side of the horse. 'Oh my back! How it hurts!' the potter cried, but his wife gently reminded him of all the glory that awaited him if only he could learn to ride the horse and then win the battle. And the potter, thinking of all that would be his if only he could lead the charge successfully, tried again and again to mount the horse. And bravo! One day he finally did it.

As soon as he mounted, the horse, one of the finest in the whole kingdom, began to race ahead at full speed in the direction of the enemy's camp with the potter seated on its back, clutching at its mane. Frightened out of his wits and fearing a terrible fall, he clung to the horse with all his might but this made the horse double its speed. And the louder he screamed 'Stop! Stop! Stop!' the faster the horse galloped on, on, it leaped, jumped, bounded and ran at full speed across hedges, bushes, plains and ditches and crossing many a winding rivers and going over little blue-green hills it came into a grove of trees beyond which was the enemy's camp. In a desperate bid to stop the horse from racing on at full speed and not willing to face the enemy, the potter stretched out a hand and caught hold of a small banyan tree with all his strength just as the horse whizzed past it. But the horse was in no mood to stop and because of the violent pull—and the soil here was quite loose— the banyan tree with all its aerial roots came off the

earth with a loud sound. But still the great charger galloped on and on like an arrow released from a bow. Like a flash of lightning it shot through the air with the potter clasping the banyan tree under his arm and riding on.

Not far away was the enemy's camp and from the watchtower the enemy took no time in spotting the horse with the strange rider. 'What on earth is this thing coming our way at full speed—a rider with a titanic tree?' cried the soldiers and soon there was great commotion in the camp.

'War! War! War! Here comes the enemy's army led by a man of great stature mounted on a mighty charger, carrying a gigantic tree that he has torn off the ground in his great rage,' cried the commander-in-chief of the enemy's camp.

This news made the king of Pappanadu, who had wanted a war, very nervous. 'What, the opponent's army is led by a man who has torn off a tree in his rage—and a banyan tree at that?' he asked nervously.

All at once the soldiers cried, 'The whole force must be strong like this man and will come charging at us, tearing up the very forest in their frenzy! They will squash us like ants with these huge trees! We can fight men but not giants! They'll all finish us! Flee, brothers, flee! This is just one man we see. Behind him comes the entire army!' Saying so, they pleaded with their king to make peace at once. The king too readily agreed to this and wrote out a letter proposing terms of peace. Then the entire army took to its heels.

At last the horse, tired from having run for such a great distance with the potter clasping at its mane with one hand and with the other hugging a tree, came to a halt on reaching the enemy's camp. The potter too, almost dead from fatigue, sighed in relief, flung away the tree and tumbled off the horse. He then sat down to rest, while the horse ate some grass. Just then he found the letter that the fleeing king had written, which he had left behind in his hurry to leave. Carefully tucking the letter in the folds of his dhoti at the waist, he heaved another sigh of relief and laughed. Then, he walked back to his village with the horse.

When the potter reached his home, he told his wife about his adventure and showed her the letter. The wife was delighted. Slapping her husband on his back, which made him hiccup, she exclaimed, 'Bravo husband! We shall go and meet the raja tomorrow morning.' And next morning, the potter, accompanied by his wife, set off for the raja's palace and on meeting him presented the letter with a great flourish.

The raja's eyes nearly popped out on reading its content. 'No war? Peace! Peace! What a great relief!' he shouted with joy. Hearing this, the young prince, who did not want to be the commander-in-chief, came running out of his palace. 'No war! No war!' he shouted as he jumped up and down with happiness. 'Now I can sing and play and eat chocolates and ice-creams without a worry!' he exclaimed. And the young princess, accompanied by the queen, came running out of their palace and clapping their hands shouted, 'Peace! Peace! Down with ugly wars!' Soon all the people of the kingdom came out too and cheered and danced and sang and clapped their hands, 'No war! We don't want a war! We want to live in peace! We hate bloodshed!' they cried.

After the rejoicing was over, the raja of Tamrapani and his subjects, who could not simply believe that their Valiant Chattee-maker of Tamrapani had single-handedly driven away the huge army of the enemy and ensured peace in their kingdom, gave him many cheers. The raja called a darbar and before a distinguished gathering of ministers, messengers, princes and princesses, and his queen, he honoured the potter and his wife with rewards of great riches, a palace and a donkey, which was once again named Tiger.

Phurruth Phurr!

A little prince and a little princess loved nothing more than to listen to stories. Their father, the king, was generally busy with the affairs of the state. And yet, whenever he found the time, he told the little prince and the little princess many, many tales of ghouls and witches, demons and wizards, princes and princesses, and kings and queens. Their mother, the queen, also told the royal children many, many stories at bedtime—stories of flying horses, clever animals, wily sorcerers, magic flutes and magic drums. But at the end of each story, the little prince and the little princess had only one thing to say, 'Another story, please! We shall not go to sleep if you do not tell us another story!' And they would scream and jump on their royal beds thrashing their arms

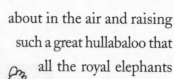

about in the air and raising
such a great hullabaloo that
all the royal elephants
and horses would start
up from their sleep
and trumpeting and
neighing, they too
would demand, 'A story!
A story! N-e-e-i-i-g-g-h-h! Tell us a story please!'
And all the members of the royal household, hearing
the cacophony would rush out of their rooms to see
what the matter was and they too would scream, 'A
story! A story! Tell us a story too!'

The king and queen, being very good royal personages,
readily fell in with the wishes of their subjects and
obliged the elephants and the horses and all the
members of the royal
household by telling
them story after story,
night after night. One night,
however, the king and the
queen found that they had
run out of their stock of
tales. The king just did not

know which new story to tell, for he had narrated almost all the stories that he had known as a boy. And his queen too had told all the stories that she had known as a girl. They simply did not know what to do. The little prince and the little princess and now every royal being, be it man or animal, just refused to go to sleep unless every night they were told new tales.

'Shall I play some music for you, my lovely children?' exhausted, the king would ask. 'Music will lull you to sleep.'

'Shall I sing a lullaby for you, my sweetie pies?' the queen would coax, but to no effect.

'No, please! Another story, please!' the royal brother and sister would shriek on the top of their voices like two thoroughly spoilt brats in need of a good spanking on their soft, plump buttocks. But really, the little prince and the princess were not spoilt imps at all! For what they asked for was not sugar candies that give toothache and ice lollops that give soar throat, but for enchanting, exciting, hair-raising, eye-popping, spine-tingling wild new tales. And that was not a bad thing at all except that there was one problem—there were no more stories.

Now, since both the king and the queen had run out of stories to tell, the constant demand of 'Another story, please!' put the king in a tight spot. He was at a loss as to what to do. So one day, the king's minister said to him, 'Your Majesty, why not hire a storyteller who could tell non-stop stories to the prince and the princess, the elephants and the horses and all of us?'

'That's it!' exclaimed the king with great relief. 'You may look overblown and plump and sloppy but aren't you clever!'

Happily that very moment the king sent a messenger to go from village to village across the length and breadth of the kingdom to look for a storyteller. Beating his drum, the messenger cried, 'The king will reward handsomely a storyteller who will not stop telling tales.'

For days and weeks the search was on for a storyteller who would not tire of telling stories. But finding one was not easy. For the people said, 'What's the use of telling tales that do not fetch us our bread? It's so much better fishing or selling vegetables or washing clothes, for that's where the money is! So much better being a fisherman or a honey-seller, a weaver or a potter, for tales will not bring us our meals!'

Finally one day, a young boy and a girl arrived at the king's court with their grandmother. 'My grandmother is the best storyteller in the world. She can tell the prince and princess as many stories as they would like to hear! But she will tell her stories if only you let us all live in the palace and look after us and feed us, for we're poor,' the children said.

The king and the queen were delighted. At once they took the little boy and girl and their grandmother in and provided them with a room in the palace that had a wonderful view and fed them and gave them fresh, clean clothes to wear. Now that Grandmother had enough leisure and no worries about feeding her grandchildren who were orphans, all day long she sat out under the flowering champaka tree or the handsome bakul tree, dreaming and listening to bird songs, and watching clouds float by in the bluest of skies. And all the while, in her mind she spun and wove incessant tales—tales of hope and wisdom, fun and adventure, love and laughter.

And every night she poured out her enchanting tales to the royal audience that listened to her enthralled. Everyone marvelled at her. So wonderful and charming were her tales that even the king and the queen began to scream and to jump and make loud demands for more tales, and when they did that they forgot they were the grown-up First Gentleman and First Lady of the kingdom. Instead, like children they

giggled and laughed and their eyes filled with wonder at Grandmother's never-ending tales.

But problems seldom come to a complete end. One night, when the royal children clamoured, 'Another story please, Grandmother!' the old lady began to fumble and to grope for words. Alas, alas! Grandmother too had come to the end of her stock. What was she going to do? Her two little grandchildren looked at her, dejected and disappointed. They knew if she could not tell any more tales, they would have to leave the palace and return to their hut. And then, they would have to take their goats and sheep to the meadow for grazing and go into the forest to collect firewood for Grandmother to cook gruel rice and roast sweet potatoes. All this fun of living in a palace, eating pulao and biryani, and playing with the prince and the princess would come to an end. Sadly they looked at their grandmother. And Grandmother too looked at her grandchildren for a long, long time. Then, a naughty smile broke across the old woman's face.

Clearing her voice and opening her silver betel-nut case and taking a puff at her hukkah—for she did smoke one which made a ghooor ghooor sound—she started on her new tale: 'There lived a flock of rose-ringed parakeets on a dancing peepal tree. And as soon as the eastern sky turned pink and gold in the first light of dawn and all the birds began to twitter, a bird flew off from the tree, making a noise like this: Phurruth phurr!' Saying so, Grandmother paused.

'And then what happened, Grandmother?' asked the little prince.

'And then another bird flew off, making a noise like this: phurruth phurr!' said Grandmother, looking very serious.

'And then what happened, Grandmother?' asked the little princess.

'And then another bird flew off, phurruth phurr!' said Grandmother.

'And then?' asked the king, his face filled with wonder.

'And then, phurruth phurr! Another bird flew away!'

'And then?' asked the queen with a look of enchantment in her eyes.

'And then, phurruth phurr! Yet another bird flew away!'

'And then?' asked the elephants and the horses.

'Phurruth phurr!'

'And then?' chorused all the members of the royal household with great excitement.

'Phurruth phurr!' replied Grandmother with a mischievous twinkle in her eyes.

This went on and on until nothing was heard except 'And then?' and 'Phurruth phurr!'

Finally, the little prince and the little princess, rubbing sleep from their eyes, asked, 'How long will this go on, Grandmother?'

And Grandmother, pinching the cheeks of her grandchildren, the boy and the girl who huddled close to her, laughed and said, 'Till all the birds are gone! Mind you, a flock may sometimes consist of a thousand birds!'

The prince and the princess yawned and fell on their

bed, deep in sleep. The king yawned and the queen yawned and all the other royal grown-ups too yawned and everyone retired for the night. Surely tomorrow night Grandmother would have another enchanting tale to tell!